FIRST FLIGHT®

*FIRST FLIGHT® is an exciting
new series of beginning readers.
The series presents titles which include songs,
poems, adventures, mysteries, and humour
by established authors and illustrators.
FIRST FLIGHT® makes the introduction to
reading fun and satisfying
for the young reader.*

*FIRST FLIGHT® is available in 4 levels
to correspond to reading development.*

Level 1 – Preschool - Grade 1
Large type, repetition of simple concepts that are perfect
for reading aloud, easy vocabulary and endearing
characters in short simple stories for the earliest reader.

Level 2 – Grade 1 - Grade 3
Longer sentences, higher level of vocabulary, repetition,
and high-interest stories for the progressing reader.

Level 3 – Grade 2 - Grade 4
Simple stories with more involved plots and a simple
chapter format for the newly independent reader.

Level 4 – Grade 3 - up (First Flight Chapter Books)
More challenging level, minimal illustrations for the
independent reader.

For Gregory
who told me I should try
another kind of pencil.

FIRST FLIGHT® is a registered trademark of Fitzhenry & Whiteside

Omar on Ice
Copyright © 1999 by Maryann Kovalski

First publication in the United States in 2000.

Fitzhenry & Whiteside acknowledges with thanks the support of the Government of Canada through its Book Publishing Industry Development Program in the publication of this title.

Design by Wycliffe Smith Design.

Printed in Canada.

10 9 8 7 6 5 4 3 2

Canadian Cataloguing in Publication Data

Kovalski, Maryann
Omar on Ice

(A first flight reader)
ISBN 1-55041-409-7 Hardcover
ISBN 1-55041-407-0 Paperback

I. Title. II. Series.

PS8571.O96J55 1998   jC813'.54   C98-931542-8
PZ8.3.K8535 Ji 1998

A First Flight® Level Two Reader

OMAR ON ICE

BY
MARYANN KOVALSKI

Fitzhenry & Whiteside • Toronto

Omar loved pictures.

When he grew up,
he was going to be an artist.

People would come
from all over.
He would paint their pictures.

Maybe they would pay him
with candy.

Omar liked red ju-jubes best.

Omar could not wait for school
tomorrow. Maybe Ms. Fudge
would hold up his picture for
the whole class to see.

But in art class, Omar just
looked at his paper.

"I don't know what to draw,"
said Omar.

"Why don't you draw
something you love?"
said Ms. Fudge.

This gave Omar an idea.
He picked up his pencil and
started to draw.

The class was quiet.
Everyone worked very hard.

Ms. Fudge looked at
Thomas' drawing.

"My, what lovely rocks, Thomas,"
said Ms. Fudge.
"Thank you," said Thomas.

Ms. Fudge looked at
Omar's drawing.

"This is wonderful, Omar!"
said Ms. Fudge.

"Look class. Look at the big rock
Omar has drawn!"

"That is not a rock," said Omar. "That is my mother."

"Oh, dear," said Ms. Fudge.

She looked at the drawing again.

"Yes, I see it. My, she is very pretty. Why don't you draw your father now?"

Ms. Fudge held up
Elsie's picture.

"Look at the pretty flower
Elsie drew," said Ms. Fudge.

Omar wished he could
draw like Elsie.

Omar threw his drawing away.
Maybe I am not good at people,
thought Omar.

I will try something else.
When he finished he was very
happy with his drawing.

"Look, Ms. Fudge! Look at
my drawing!" said Omar.
Ms. Fudge looked. She smiled
a very big smile.

"Your father will love his picture,
Omar," said Ms. Fudge.

"But it is not my father,"
said Omar.
"It is my cat, Willow."

Ms. Fudge looked at
the drawing again.

"Oh, yes. Silly me.
It is a very good cat."

Ms. Fudge walked away.

"It is not a very good cat,"
said Omar to Thomas.
"I am a bad artist."

"Maybe it is your pencil,"
said Elsie.

"Maybe you need another
kind of pencil," said Thomas.

"It is not my pencil.
It is me," said Omar.

The bell rang. It was time for
recess.

They were all happy because
the pond was frozen. It was a
perfect day for skating.

Soon, everyone was on the ice,
even Ms. Fudge. Everyone,
except Omar.

"Why are you sitting, Omar?"
asked Thomas. "You are the best
skater in the class."

"I do not care if I am the best
skater. I want to be the best
artist," said Omar.

He watched the others sadly.

Elsie skated by.
She did not skate as well as she
drew flowers.

She fell down hard on the ice.
Omar helped her up.
"Rats," she said. "I am
a bad skater."

"Maybe it is your skates," said Omar.

"It is not my skates," said Elsie. "It is me. I am a bad skater."

"You are trying too hard," said Omar. "Just have fun when you skate. Then you will see how easy it is."

"Now watch this," said Omar.

"Hold your arms like this,
and don't be afraid. It's
easy when you don't worry."

Omar skated this way and that.

He went up on the toes of his skates and whirled in a circle.

He skated forwards and backwards.

28

Sometimes he glided
slowly like a bird in the sky.

Sometimes he raced
quickly like a fast car.

He skated from one end
of the pond to the other.

Soon Omar forgot all about
being a bad artist.

He was having too much fun.

When he jumped high
in the air everyone cheered.

"Look at Omar!" said Thomas.
"Look at the ice!" said Elsie.

Everyone looked.

On the ice were
beautiful lines wherever
Omar had skated.

"Look at the turtle
that Omar drew!"
said Elsie.

"Look at the bird
that Omar drew!"
said Thomas.

"Look! Omar's mother!"
said Ms. Fudge.

It was true.
Omar had drawn many
beautiful pictures on the ice.

Even he could see
how good his drawings were.

"I was right" said Thomas.
"You just needed
a different kind of pencil!"

Other Books in the
First Flight® series

Level 1 – Preschool - Grade 1
Fishes in the Ocean *written by* Maggee Spicer
and Richard Thompson, *illustrated by* Barbara Hartmann
Then & Now *written by* Richard Thompson, *illustrated*
by Barbara Hartmann

Level 2 – Grade 1 - Grade 3
Flying Lessons *written and illustrated by* Celia Godkin
Jingle Bells *written and illustrated by* Maryann Kovalski
Rain, Rain *written and illustrated by* Maryann Kovalski

Level 3 – Grade 2 - Grade 4
Andrew's Magnificent Mountain of Mittens *written*
by Deanne Lee Bingham *and illustrated by* Kim La Fave
Andrew, Catch That Cat! *written by* Deanne Lee
Bingham, *illustrated by* Kim La Fave

Level 4 – Grade 3 - up (First Flight Chapter Books)
The Money Boot *written by* Ginny Russell,
illustrated by John Mardon
Fangs & Me *written by* Rachna Gilmore,
illustrated by Gordon Sauvé
More Monsters in School *written by* Martyn Godfrey,
illustrated by John Mardon